A Soul FOR Sale

by Chris Linton

DORRANCE
PUBLISHING CO
EST. 1920
PITTSBURGH, PENNSYLVANIA 15238

Dorrance Publishing Co
585 Alpha Drive
Suite 103
Pittsburgh, PA 15238
Visit our website at *www.dorrancebookstore.com*

ISBN: 978-1-6480-4431-1
eISBN: 978-1-6480-4532-5

A Soul for Sale

*C*hapter 1

On a chilly fall morning with a light mist in the air, a stranger walked up to the crowd. To many of the guests he looked like a homeless man. This man was 6'7" tall with a muscular frame. He was dressed in worn blue jeans, dirty tennis shoes, and a suit jacket that surprisingly was somewhat clean. His long brown shoulder-length hair pulled back into a ponytail while he sported a five-o'clock shadow. He introduced himself as John Nolan.

Once the service was done, the stranger stayed behind just looking at the grave of one Christopher St. George. A man in his middle fifties walked up to ask the stranger if he knew his son Chris. Perhaps from the war. This man was dressed in a black suit, shiny black shoes, hair neatly trimmed. This man had a sadness in his eyes—his second son was dead.

John shook his hand, offering his condolences, simply saying, "Yes, I knew your son, he was a good man," then walked away.

March 31st, 1972, Christopher St. George was born to hardworking parents in a small farming community in southern Minnesota. He was your average run-of-the-mill child. Intelligent but wild, rebellious. After high school he joined the United States Marine Corps. Went to boot camp and immediately after, to officer training. Life was good. Then he was ordered to war. Then another. It was his job to send his men into battle knowing some would only return home in a box draped with a flag. This wore heavy on his soul. He began to drink heavily, trying to fight off his demons.

After being deployed to yet another war, another foreign land, he had had enough. He could no longer fight for something he didn't absolutely believe in, fight for a man he would never meet. He was done. Instead of remaining back at base barking out orders via radio while others fought and died, he led his men into battle. Christopher St. George died that day. He was 35 years old. John Nolan was born.

John made his way back to the States. Got a birth certificate, Social Security card, and a driver's license. An easy task if you knew the right people, which he did. He found an apartment, a job, and blended into society. Little known to the rest of the world, Chris had forged many valuable contacts during his time in the service of his country, contacts that had allowed him to amass great wealth. Wealth that came at a great price. He had sold his soul. He provided weapons to enemies of his country. That was why Christopher had to die. He had betrayed his country. It might seem immoral and you're right, it is. But I had believed I had already sold my soul for the things I did "for the service of my country."

Kill people because they stood in the way of so-called progress. Progress that was all about money. So I made my own progress and it didn't bother me; after all, I was just doing the same thing they were. Making money. Money that would make my life better, so I thought. It just added more demons.

*C*hapter 2

Don't get me wrong, I kept some of the millions I acquired but most I gave to charity, hoping I could buy back my soul. If I could do some good with it, help those that actually needed it, I would begin to feel better. I didn't.

It's funny how life changes one's beliefs. As a young officer, I gave 110 percent. I believed in what I was told and in what I was doing, but as time went on, wars kept coming. More young men and women under my command died. Good soldiers who gave their lives because that was what their country asked of them. Good soldiers who would not see or hold their loved ones again. That was when I began to think differently.

I was sitting in a dimly lit bar on the east side of Chicago, drowning myself in whiskey, when a man struck up a conversation with me. He was in his mid-fifties, well dressed with tanned skin. Definitely not someone you'd expect to find in a bar like this one. He introduced himself as Mr. Simmons. We exchanged pleasantries, but I really wasn't in the mood for conversation. Noticing my demeanor, he excused himself. After a couple weeks of trying to drown out my demons, all the while this Mr. Simmons was there. Every day and every night like clockwork.

Drunk and looking for a fight, I walked up to him and asked him what his problem was. Why was he always hanging around? He said he knew what I was going through and could possibly be of help. First thought I had was *Help with what? I don't need your help.* But we sat and talked for hours. Turned out he was former military, an enlisted man. And he felt the same way I did. Definitely my kind of person. He knew he had me hook, line, and sinker.

At first all I had to do was misplace a couple crates of M-4s. And that was easy since I had once saved the requisition's officer's son. Not on the battlefield. A young man was getting bested in a bar brawl several years earlier while I was stationed at Camp Pendleton in Oceanside, California. He had danced with the wrong woman and her husband didn't take kindly to her dancing with another man, so he and five of his friends dragged the boy out to the parking lot and proceeded to beat him. Punching and kicking him. Normally I wouldn't have stepped in but he was a Marine. He was a brother.

I told the men he had had enough, he learned his lesson and was unlikely to repeat the mistake. The biggest of them came at me, swung, and missed. This man was 6'6" and easily weighed a good 250 pounds. He was dressed in a white t-shirt that was too tight. He had a muscular build, but I could tell he liked to drink from his beer gut. One solid punch to his kidney put him down. The next man, tall and lanky, dropped like a sack of potatoes once his knee was smashed backwards. The others decided to leave when they saw what I had done to their buddies with little effort. I picked the boy up, bloody and broken, and drove him to the hospital, where he was immediately admitted. After that I didn't see him again. I had been drinking myself and had not wanted to deal with a bunch of questions, so I left. I didn't know his name and I really didn't care. About a year later, a young man came up to me and said he was that boy from the bar and wanted to thank me for saving his life. He had scars on his face but otherwise looked in good shape. Especially for the beating he took. I didn't leave my name that night, so I'm not sure how he tracked me down. But had he not I wouldn't have met a man years later that would turn out to be his father.

I was compensated $25,000 for that deal. It was the first of many lucrative deals with my new partner.

Chapter 3

After about a year of making good money, I moved my sights to bigger game. With the contacts I had made while working with my partner and those from my own time in the service, I was soon moving plane loads of weapons to various destinations around the globe. After five years or so, I had amassed nearly 500 million U.S. dollars. That's when I got busted; my former partner had set me up, believing that I had stolen from him when I cut him out. After a lengthy investigation, the government set up a sting. By this time I was greedy. I didn't care who I did business with. I was charged with arms dealing, and when my fingerprints came back to a man that was dead, I was also charged with desertion and treason. At best I could hope to spend the rest of my life in a military prison.

It never went to trial. Certain high-ranking government officials figured that with the contacts I had made from years of arms dealing, I was in a position to help them. I was debriefed. Hell, I figured selling out those who had made me rich was better than life in prison, or worse. I was able to keep selling arms as long as I worked with the government by feeding them information.

Like I told you earlier, war is profitable. Wars are fought over territory, natural resources, religion, and many other things, and it's called "politics," it's called "progress." Everyone wants to be on top of the food chain.

My plan was simple, meet and deal only in one region at a time. How did I choose the region in which to work? Well, that was the easy part. I was told where to go, where the government wanted or needed intel.

In the past when I was on my own, I simply sold to anyone and everyone. Anyone who had enough money. I mean, why only supply weapons to one side and not the other? There's no fair play in that. One side would win outright and the other, if they were lucky, wouldn't be wiped out of extinction. But now it was different; I had a boss again. Ironic. I worked for the United States of America in the beginning and because of their politics, their political agenda, I faked my own death and went into business for myself doing the exact same thing. Only difference was all the profit went into my bank account. And now after much success, I was once again working for the entity I had learned to distrust and hate.

At first I was grateful. I felt extremely fortunate, even lucky that I wasn't going to spend the rest of my life in a 6-by-8-foot prison cell at Leavenworth, or disappear altogether. Whether you believe it or not, our government can make someone vanish. All governments, if threatened, have this ability. The trick now was to survive and under no circumstances let my clients find out that I sold them out to save my own skin.

For my first mission, my "employer," a term I use lightly, needed intel on a specific group in the Middle East. So I made contact with my people in that area, set up a meeting with the militant group's leader, and brokered a deal. Only trouble was, before that's all I did. Set a meeting, made a deal, and delivered the agreed-upon goods. But now as part of my job, I needed to build relationships that went far beyond my realm of expertise.

I had to learn quickly customs for each group targeted, languages, who's who, etc., etc. If I messed up, if I offended the wrong person, I was a dead man. Only this time there would be no coming back, no new identity.

What did I care what their politics were? What did I care what the reasons for slaughtering each other were? Hell, I knew the reasons, it's the same everywhere, in every war. This land belongs to my people. No, this land belongs to my people. Your religion is different than mine. It's usually a "he said she said" situation. And sometimes you just have people that want to kill you for no reason at all, other than they had nothing better to do. I did have a tagalong; my shadow was a muscular man. Special Forces through and through. 6'2", muscular but lean at the same time. His hair high and tight, a Special Forces tattoo on his upper-left bicep. His skin was tanned dark and rough like leather. This man had been on missions all around the world. He could kill with precision and skill. Someone who, for better or worse, was assigned to me. You have to understand, by this point I was a millionaire. I couldn't just sign the "contract" with the government, so to speak, and disappear. I had the resources. I had the knowledge. But they wouldn't let that happen, I already had built business relationships with many if not most of the most notorious terror groups and military leaders of the known world and even some in the little-known world. Small villages in the middle of nowhere, tribe against tribe. That sort of thing. It wasn't all bad having my new shadow. He already was an expert on many of the customs and the what-not of many places and regions that we were sent into. That was the advantage; the disadvantage was now I had to explain why I no longer worked alone. Oh, yeah, a cover story was ready and waiting for me to memorize before the deal was offered.

Chapter 4

Year after year, I did what my government told me to do. Went where they wanted, when they wanted. I barely made it out alive more than a few times. But that's life. We take risks, some necessary, some not. We always hope it will turn out good. Sometimes it does and sometimes it doesn't, sometimes you just run out of luck. If you have ever been in a situation like this, then you know at some point you will be of no more use and at that moment you are dead. See, it looks bad if a world leader assassinates another world leader. What they do is find a reason to invade another land and start a war. That way if the war-torn country's leader is killed, it's considered a casualty of war, collateral damage. Also by gaining intel on each specific group, you can make the decision on which one is the lesser evil. Provide arms to that one and hope for the best.

But what my government didn't know was with each deal I made for them, I also made one on the side that would at some point be very beneficial to me. For the time when I decided I had danced enough for the puppet master. The problem with complex planning is there is too much stuff you must remember. The position I was in, I needed simplicity. I didn't require a whole lot to accomplish my exit plan. Early on, I knew that one day I would need to execute my handler in order to move on.

Yes, they said that by "working with them" I would not be tried for treason. The world would not know that I faked my own death. The world would never know of the crimes against my fellow people. It wasn't the world I was afraid of, it was my family. A family that thought I had died many years before. I just couldn't bear the thought of hurting them like that. I didn't want them to know the child they raised could become such a monster. That was my primary reason for agreeing to do what I did.

Within the first two years of my newly landed job, I had my plan in place. All I had to do was contact my most trusted associates and lucky for me, they just happened to be within the initial ten places I was ordered to go. It was still tricky and dangerous. I had to be very discreet on how I went about contacting these people. After all, if my shadow caught on the jig was up. I would have probably been executed on the spot. I mean really, do you think they would spend taxpayer money to fly me back just to stand trial? No, I didn't think so either.

*C*hapter 5

Before Chris died he met a young woman. A woman much younger than himself. Jasmine was 22 years old, she was the most beautiful woman he had ever laid eyes on. Blonde with a smile that immediately attracted him. He knew at that moment he had to talk to her. The two became friends and before long were inseparable. Their relationship was purely platonic. Though she was still special to him. She gave him something no other person on earth was able to give. She gave him peace. When they were together his demons were at bay. Several months after meeting her he was deployed yet again, he didn't want to go, he didn't want to leave her. Leaving her meant his demons would likely return, and they did. He was again at war both for his country and with himself.

Chapter 6

Soldiers drink. Soldiers see ugliness most people can't even fathom. Many a soldier loses their fight with their demons. Too many by their own hand. Chris lost his fight too. Though he did not take his own life. He did die. But another rose to take his fight on. Chris and John wanted to be better people. Even though Chris wasn't able to accomplish that goal, John took it up for him. Unfortunately Chris' demons were passed on to John. We can change our name but we cannot change who we are. I used to think like that but I know better now.

All it took was a simple bat of my eye at one specific person. That was the signal. Not even my shadow would be suspicious of me blinking. That one insignificant eye movement told my contact that the person next to me was the intended target. Only to be taken out when they the time was right. And not until then. You see, being an arms dealer, a dealer of death, you must always have safeguards in place. After all, it's a dangerous occupation. Before I would walk into any situation, everything was always preset. Everyone knew their role.

People that walk into dangerous situations had better have an out just in case things go awry. Some of my competitors lasted, only because they thought like I did. Some did not. They were cocky, they thought they could control the situation, they thought they could talk their way out of anything. They thought wrong.

A bat of my eye let one person know one thing. That person's job had two parts. First and foremost signal the next person, secondly watch my back. Same with the next person, signal the next and watch my back and so on and so forth. When I went into any situation I had a minimum of six people on the ground, each with their own role to play. And that was just in the immediate area. Snipers were posted at various points along the planned route. Everyone was a professional. We wanted to make it out alive and we wanted that almighty dollar. It was business. We didn't care if John Q. Public lived or not. To us they were acceptable loses, casualties of war. After all, that is how we were trained to think.

Chapter 7

After Chris left he knew he would never be the same, that's when he began to devise his plan. The plan for his death and for his resurrection. He arranged for a body to be at a specific location. This body was mutilated beyond recognition. Its sole purpose was to take Chris' place in death, Chris' dog tags were the only way to identify the body. As long as his dog tags were there, the military would believe it was, in fact, Christopher St. George. Phase one complete.

The next part was a little more tricky; after all, we were in the middle of a warzone. A way out without being caught or killed by either side. If the enemy caught us, we would likely have been tortured then beheaded. If the U.S. caught us, I for one would be tried for treason and desertion since many of my contacts were not of American descent. Neither option sounded favorable to me. I had to be smart, plan every little thing out to the finest detail.

Phase two was secure. Safe passage through a very hostile and unforgiving environment. That meant bribing many officials on both sides. And even then you couldn't be 100% sure that they wouldn't take your money, then double cross you. I know it sounds stupid, but even though I had committed the most atrocious and heinous crimes against my fellow man I always, always carried my bible with me everywhere I went. As I believed God would protect me against my enemies and my demons.

Fast forward four months. Christopher St. George was dead and John Nolan had risen from his ashes with a renewed hope for life, for change. When I first got back to the States, everything was going my way. I had gotten sober. Met a woman that would later become my wife. But it wasn't all rainbows and unicorn's. When I first met Kendra, she was married. Our relationship began as friendship. Kendra made me feel the same way Jasmine had. We would laugh and just hang out. Kendra was even in height to Jasmine; she had reddish brown hair that stretched to the middle of her back. She was petite. She was beautiful. After about a year of dating, Kendra's husband wanted to work things out. I had fallen in love with her by this point but did not want to be the reason a marriage ended, so I left. I moved from the beach back to my home state. Not long after, Kendra left her husband and moved halfway across the United States to be with me.

Little did I know just a few short years later she would be gone. Taken from me. My demons really came out of the woodwork then. I dove straight to the bottom of every bottle I could find. Nearly a year after her death, I found myself really wanting a change. My emotions were all over the place. I was thinking about things I hadn't thought about in nearly thirty years. Remembering things I thought were long gone. Distant memories from a past life.

So now it has been a year and I still grieved for my wife, but I am ready to start dating again. But the problem with that, John, just like Chris, will always try and get her, all of the women he meets, naked as fast as he can. If I can get her into bed right away, then sorry, you're no one I want to be with. Probably just another way I am selling my soul.

I have been all over the globe, seen many places, met many people. I have lived the life of a gypsy. It suited my adventurous nature. Then I reached a turning point, the proverbial fork in the road if you will. I was pushing 50 and even though I had lost my wife, I still had hopes of finding someone that would love me and I would love her. I wanted to settle down. Buy a house on the lake. Live out the rest of my days being happy. I would take being content at this point.

My contact was an Israeli man, seventy-three years old, olive skin, graying hair that most of the time was unkempt. He walked with a slight limp but never used a cane or walking stick because he said, "It makes me feel like an old person and a cripple." Muhammad always wore garb that fit the region we worked in. He spent endless hours researching for each of his roles. He is a true perfectionist.

My second contact was a woman named Maria. She spoke at least five languages, she stood at a whopping 5 feet 1 inch, but don't let her size fool you. I myself would think twice about going toe to toe with her. She was trained in the martial arts and her size made her swift.

Maria's husband, Juan, was my explosives expert. When you needed a distraction, there was no one better. He, like her, was small in stature, but equally deadly when it came to hand-to-hand combat. Juan only spoke his native language. Most of my associates were tan or olive skinned and that came in useful in many parts of the world. They were able to blend as if they belonged there.

Chapter 8

To get here I've traveled a long hard road, now is the time for this journey to end so I can begin the next one. I've spent so much time with this shadow of mine, been through so much together, I'm actually going to miss having him around, but it's time for him to go. We are headed back to where it all began.

The bullet hit him left-middle forehead....